Lug and the Giant Storks

OXFORD
UNIVERSITY PRESS

Biff and Wilma were making a treacle cake – and a big, sticky mess! Biff stirred the mixture so hard it went all over Wilma.

'Oops!' she said. 'Sorry!'

'I think you need a bigger bowl,' Kipper said helpfully. 'How about that wok?'

But Wilma wasn't listening. She was trying to clear up the mess.

Floppy helped by licking the drops from the table.

Biff went to get Wilma a clean T-shirt.

'Why don't you use that wok, Wilma?' Kipper said again. Then he cried, 'Why don't any of you ever listen to me?'

I wish they'd listen to him, too, thought Floppy.

The key on Floppy's collar started to glow.

Suddenly Wilma, Kipper, and Floppy were whisked into a vortex of dazzling colours and lights. They were spinning round and round, faster and faster…

At last they stopped spinning and…

'Wow! We're in a space wok!' Kipper shouted.

It was true. They were in a big, silver, sparkling, flying wok. Kipper and Floppy looked out of the window in excitement. Wilma hid. She didn't like heights.

Kipper pointed ahead. 'Look at that enormous planet,' he said. 'Hey – I think we're going to land.'

The space wok landed with a bump, and a big slide whizzed to the ground. Floppy and Kipper slid down.

'Wheee!' shouted Kipper. 'Coming to explore, Wilma?'

Wilma peered out of the window and shook her head.

'No thanks,' she said.

'Wait for me, Floppy,' called Kipper.

The two of them started to explore. Suddenly they heard a funny beeping sound coming towards them. It got louder and louder. Above them was an enormous space stork!

Kipper gasped. 'Run, Floppy!' he yelled.

They hid behind a rock.

The space stork flew closer, still beeping. Then it swooped down and picked up the wok, with Wilma still inside!

Kipper and Floppy watched in horror as the stork flew off, carrying the wok, and Wilma, to the top of a very tall tree. What were they going to do now?

'Come back!' Kipper yelled at the top of his voice.

Suddenly a strange little man appeared. 'You're wasting your time,' he said. 'They'll never hear you. I've been waving my flag at them for hundreds of years and they've never spotted me.'

'Who are you?' Kipper asked.

'Upperty Downerty Hopperty Skipperty Flipperty Spinnerty Jiggerty Lug's the name. But you can call me Lug,' said the little man. 'I'm a space elf. What can I do for you?'

'My friend's in the space stork's nest,' Kipper said sadly. 'I've got to rescue her.'

While Kipper told Lug what had happened, Floppy sniffed at the ground. What was that interesting smell? He wandered off to find out.

Lug wasn't worried about Wilma. 'Those space storks only want to play,' he said.

But Wilma wasn't having a good time at all.

Floppy had found the smell. It was coming from a bubble puddle. He bent over to look at himself, and his ears dipped in to the water.

Suddenly – ZING! Floppy's ears were huge! The puddle must be magic. But it didn't last long.

'Do you think it would work for me?' asked Kipper.

'Only if you're under a hundred years old,' replied Lug.

So, Kipper dipped his foot into the puddle and – ZING! His shoe grew enormous.

Kipper had an idea. He jumped into the puddle and splashed himself all over. He started to grow and grow. 'It's working!' he said happily.

A little voice called to him. It was Lug. 'Take me with you, please,' he said. 'I'd love to meet those space storks at last.'

Kipper scooped him up in his giant hand and carried on growing.

The space storks were very surprised to see the giant Kipper. But they didn't want to let Wilma go.

'Leave it to me,' said Lug. He jumped into the nest and began to dance and sing.

The three storks beeped with delight.

Meanwhile Wilma jumped into Kipper's hand, just as he started to shrink again.

Lug leaned out of the nest and threw his flag down to Kipper.

'Thanks to you, I don't need this any more,' he called.

Kipper pointed at the key round Floppy's neck. 'The key's glowing,' he said.

We're going! thought Floppy.

They landed back in the Robinson's kitchen. A bowl of treacle puffer pop cake was on the table. Everyone wanted the first piece.

'No,' said Wilma. 'Kipper has the first piece for rescuing me.'

'Yes,' agreed Kipper, smiling. 'Who's the giant round here anyway?'

He dug into his pocket, pulled out Lug's flag, and stuck it on top.

'Hooray!' they all cheered.

OXFORD
UNIVERSITY PRESS

Great Clarendon Street, Oxford OX2 6DP

Oxford University Press is a department of the University of Oxford.
It furthers the University's objective of excellence in research, scholarship,
and education by publishing worldwide in

Oxford New York

Auckland Cape Town Dar es Salaam Hong Kong Karachi
Kuala Lumpur Madrid Melbourne Mexico City Nairobi
New Delhi Shanghai Taipei Toronto

With offices in

Argentina Austria Brazil Chile Czech Republic France Greece
Guatemala Hungary Italy Japan Poland Portugal Singapore
South Korea Switzerland Thailand Turkey Ukraine Vietnam

Oxford is a registered trade mark of Oxford University Press in the UK and in certain other countries

British Library Cataloguing in Publication Data available
ISBN-13: 978-019-272659-9
ISBN-10: 0-19-272659-5
3 5 7 9 10 8 6 4 2
Printed in China